A
FISH
TALE

or, THE LITTLE ONE
THAT GOT AWAY

LEO YERXA

A GROUNDWOOD BOOK

DOUGLAS & McINTYRE

VANCOUVER / TORONTO

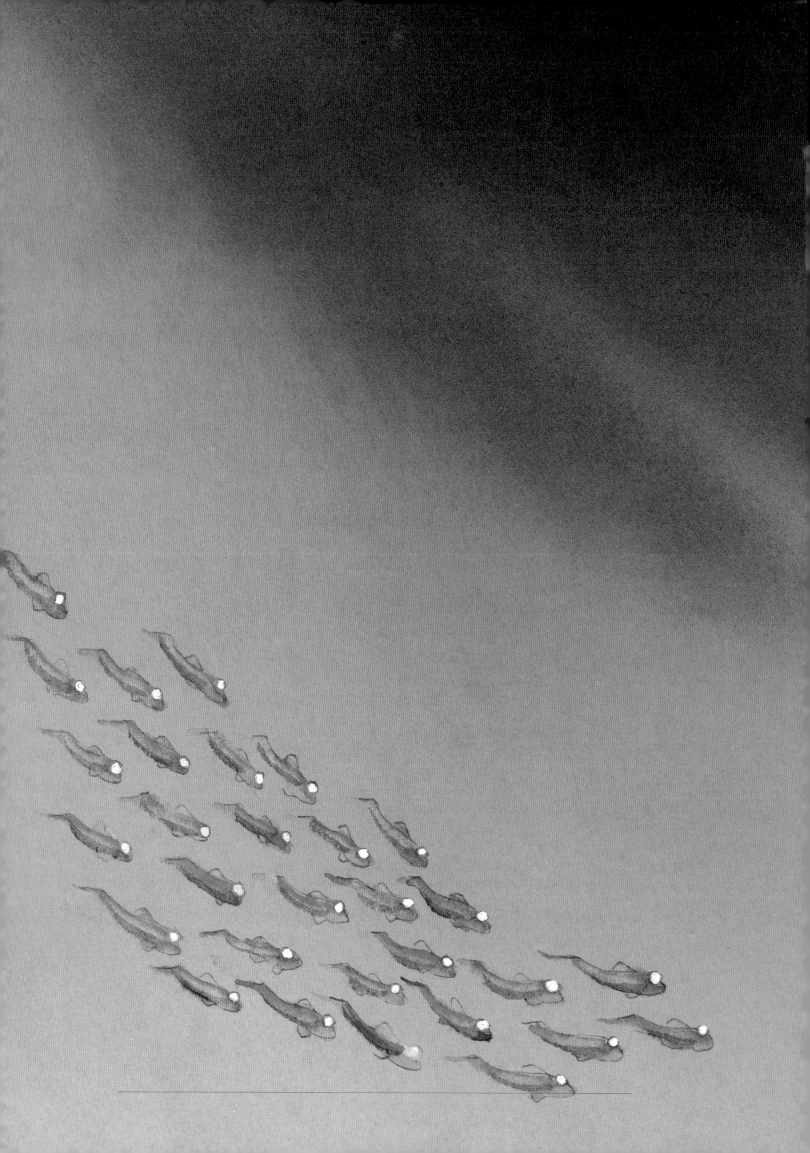

F OR MARILYN

 ALES were told in the depths of the great mystical body of water—far beneath the darkness where a fisherman's eyes could not see; down past the slimy gray rocks and green swaying weeds, where grew the garden of dreams. Grass wove its way around the twisted roots and gnarled branches of a giant hollow log, casting stringy shadows. From far above a single beam of light made its way past the rocks, weeds, roots and through the hollow log, lighting up the sands.

The whole garden was alive with color. There were fish shaped like stars and as bright, too. There were orange ones, red ones and blue ones, fat ones and flat ones darting to and fro. There were snails and dead scales with a rainbow hue, and tiny minnows that could set the night aglow.

I was in dart school. Days began with darting practice. We darted here, we darted there, we darted to one end of the garden, then to the other. In formation we dashed to the top of the garden, turned quickly and charged down toward the crystal sands. The objective was to turn upward again at the last instant.

Of course, dart school did have its failures, and I was one. A nose full of sand was more than enough to flunk darting.

Every day I would swim home from school with the fear and worries of failing darting weighing heavy on my mind. Don't get me wrong. I did like some things about school. Fantastic tales told by old, gray and dingy fuddie-duddies about other worlds, other dimensions, rivers of gold, seas of diamonds, even oceans of jewels, with humans that could swallow you whole.

Some said the stories were all true. Others said they were all lies, told to us so we would imagine the worst. One school of thought was that the stories could come true if you believed. There were stories of demons and gods, hooks, cooks and fishing rods. They sent a shiver to my tail. There were no such things as whales, and why did they always call me Small Fry anyway? I hurried on home.

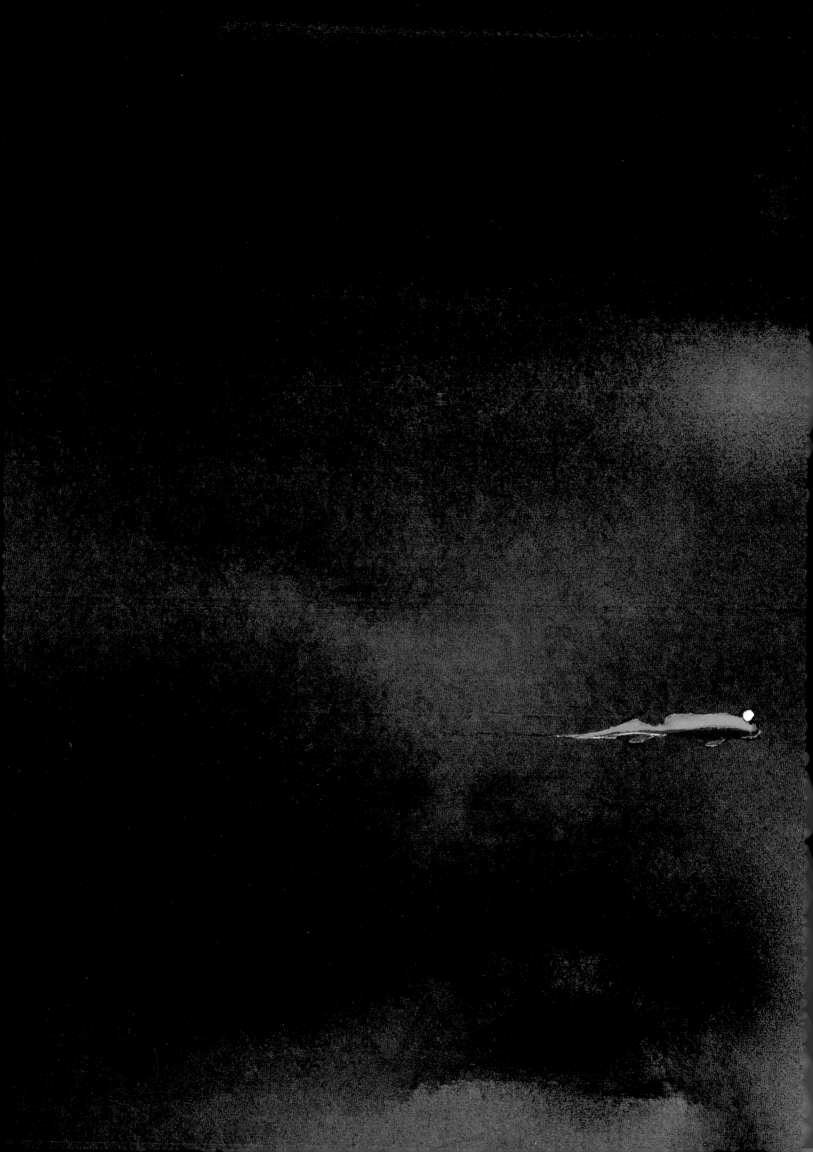

Homework done, I lay in bed thinking. Was there really a sun? I so wanted to believe. Dart school was boring, and I was just not very good at it. What lay past the slimy gray rocks? Where did that ray of light come from? And if God did make all fish equal, why were some long and others short, some big and others small? Did it begin with one big splash? And what of God? Was he a cod, or was he a she and really a bass? Was heaven above or was it below? If I died I wouldn't know which way to go.

I loved those stories, even though they left me swimming in a sea of confusion.

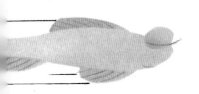

There I was trapped between failing dart school and the stories that I loved so dearly. If I could just prove that the stories were real, my life would be a tale come true. Some said that you had to get hooked to get high or life would pass you by. Beyond the slimy gray rocks were the hooks, so they said, but just who were they anyway? If I dared a swim by the edge to have a look, I could tell others about it, maybe write a book.

One morning on my way to dart school, I related my troubles and woes to a passerby who said he had been to the sky. He volunteered to swim with me to the edge to have a look at a hook.

Couldn't hurt, I thought, so I replied, "Why not?" Thoughts of dart school disappeared with the last specks of sand as I swam through the giant log into the murky waters above.

The water became darker and dirtier as we swam toward the slimy gray rocks. Jack was the name of my newfound friend.

It seemed like hours before we reached the rocks. By that time Jack had me convinced that we were headed straight to heaven with all his talk about bright shiny hooks, flies and live bait and the worms he once ate. I was tiring and lagging far behind. Jack looked back with a grin on his chin and mumbled something that sounded like Small Fry.

We swam on past the rocks and into the brightest light I had ever seen. The water seemed to go on forever. It filled me with joy. I did somersaults and flips as I yelled out, "So where are the hooks, flies and bait?"

"You'll be seeing them soon enough," Jack said with a smile. "Might even be one your size, Small Fry...I mean, Walleye."

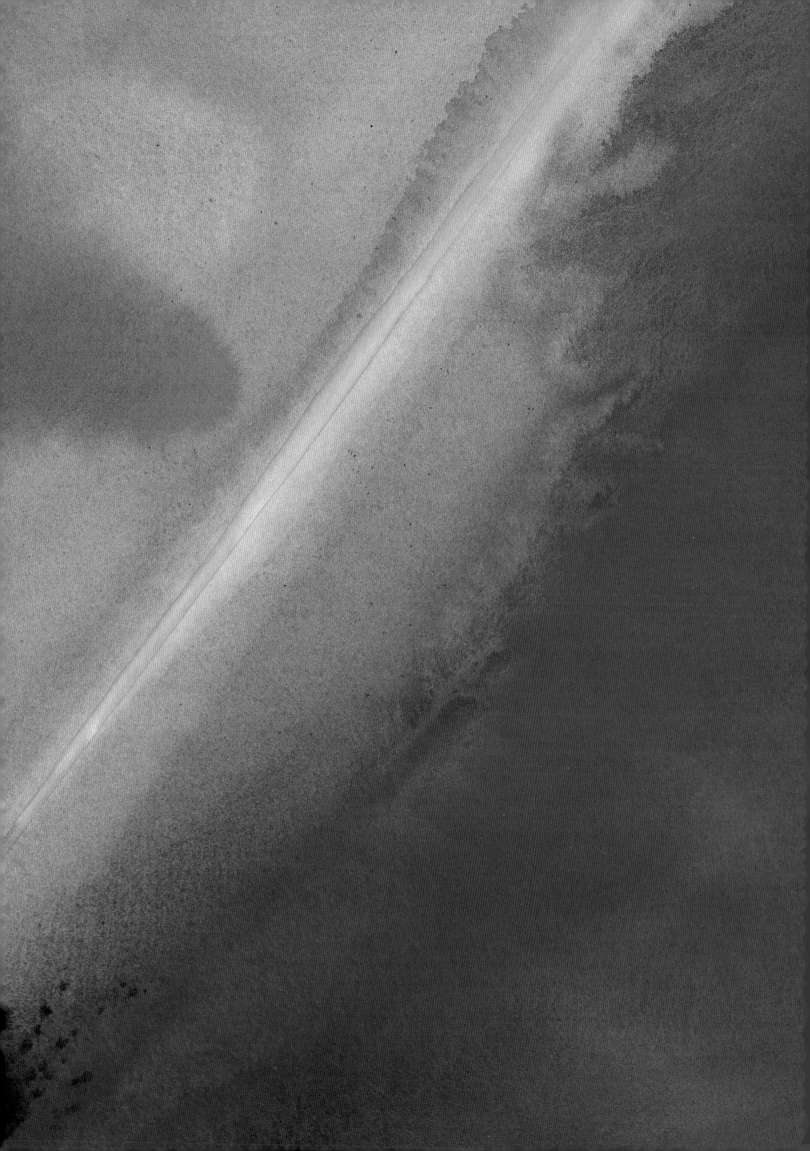

So we waited—all morning and not so much as a sight of a hook of any size. Jack strongly suggested that if we saw one my size I should give it a nibble. Finally a long hook came by.

"Jack," I said, "it's your size. You could almost swallow it whole." But Jack, being so kind, insisted that I should have the first bite.

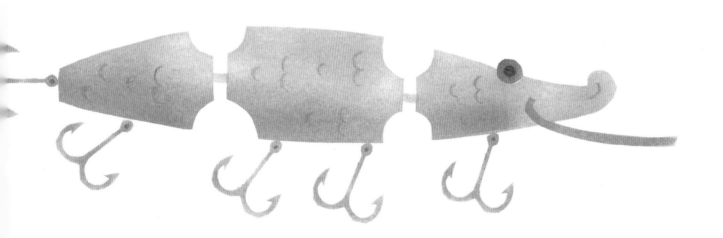

And then, "Here comes a tiny one now, kid," he yelled. "Swallow it hook, line and sinker and you'll be on your way to heaven, you little stin— I mean, thinker."

I darted at the hook with all the might I could muster. I swiped at it, but in my excitement I missed. However, my tail did touch the hook. It was sharp and pointy and cut into my fin.

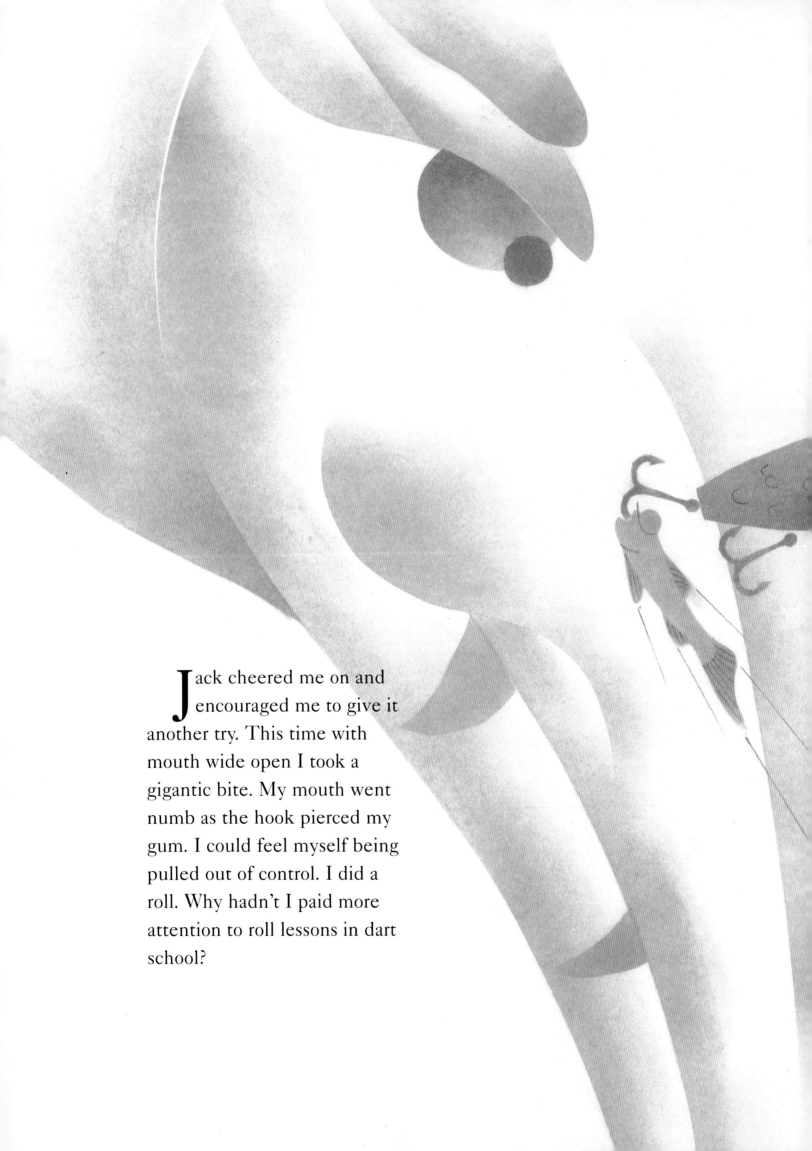

Jack cheered me on and encouraged me to give it another try. This time with mouth wide open I took a gigantic bite. My mouth went numb as the hook pierced my gum. I could feel myself being pulled out of control. I did a roll. Why hadn't I paid more attention to roll lessons in dart school?

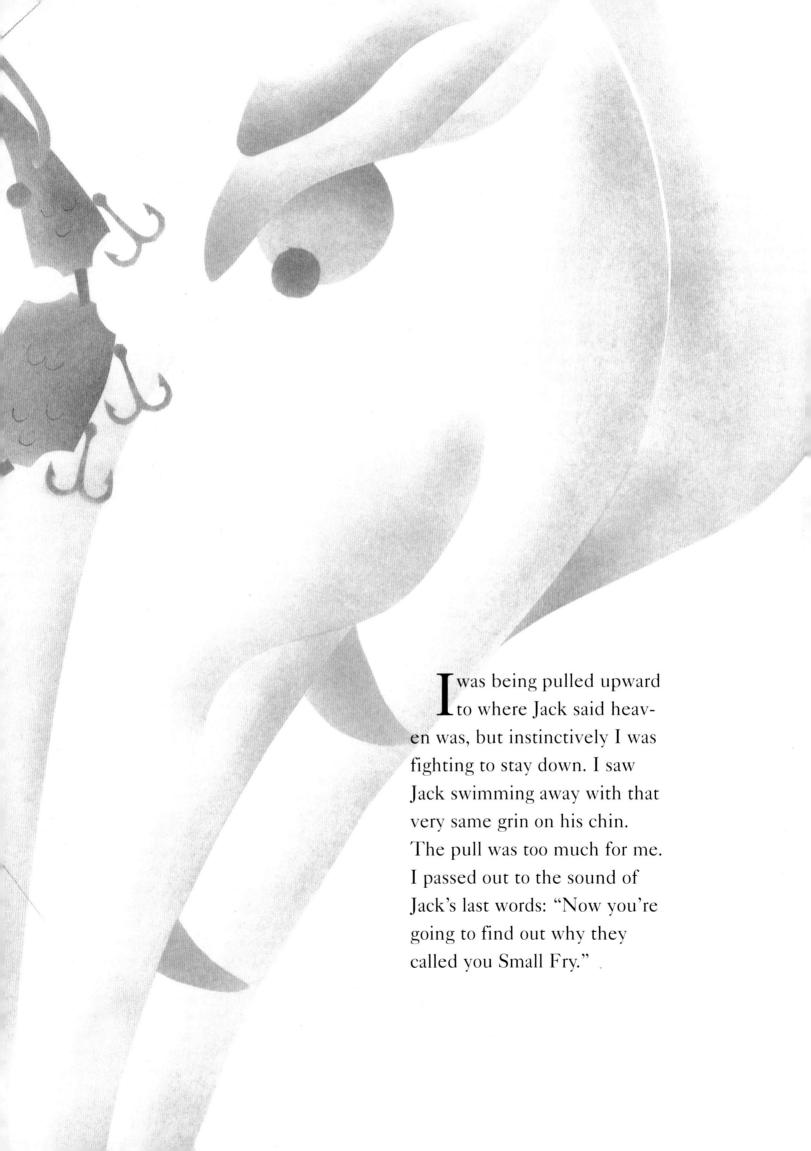

I was being pulled upward to where Jack said heaven was, but instinctively I was fighting to stay down. I saw Jack swimming away with that very same grin on his chin. The pull was too much for me. I passed out to the sound of Jack's last words: "Now you're going to find out why they called you Small Fry."

I came to in the air, gasping for water. Two huge eyes were staring down at me. Above the eyes was a hat full of hooks. Below the eyes was a huge nose with a crook and two large clumps of hair, and a mouth big enough to swallow me whole. It was bad enough that I did not even know if God was a cod, but—oh, no!—my worst nightmare had come true. Could he be a fisherman? Did he or she— God, I mean—answer small-fry prayers? I screamed at the top of my voice, "Dear God, take this hook out of my mouth. Put me back in the water, please, and I'll never do this again, I promise you."

E ven before the words were completely out of my mouth, the hook was, too. The fisherman threw me into the air and yelled, "You're too small to fry." As I sailed through the air, I glanced up at the sky and saw the sun and the trees. The sky was so blue, it was almost green. The trees were so green, they were almost blue. The great mystical body of water reflected the sky back to itself to protect the magical garden below. It was just like the stories said.

I hit the water with a tremendous crash, skipped across the waves, came to an abrupt stop and slipped beneath the surface.

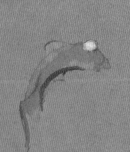

With flippers flipping, tail waving and fins flapping, I raced to the deep. I glanced back over my shoulder just long enough to see Jack fighting with a hook. From the surface I heard the fisherman's last words: "Here's one for the pan, Stan."

I darted past the slimy gray rocks, through the weeds and grass, the hollow log and out the other end. My heart raced. Home was just around the bend. Attending dart school, I thought. What a sensible thing to do. Knowing that the stories were true gave me a wonderful feeling. But could I ever tell anyone where I had gone and what I had done? No one would believe me, and would there be a punishment too great for a kid? Shattered wits and a torn fin were not proof that other dimensions existed. It could only prove me a fool.

Should I tell the story to the whole garden? Should I keep it a secret? Would I have to explain the disappearance of that fish named Jack? Dare I tell anyone that I knew God answered prayers no matter what kind of fish you were?

I decided to keep every last detail of the whole unbelievable tale a secret.

As for Jack, well! I found out that he had been wanted by the authorities in several ponds for his involvement in getting other fish hooked.

Now time has passed, and I'm an old, gray and dingy fuddie-duddie myself—and, I might add, a teacher of darting. My book, *The Little One That Got Away*, is required reading in dart schools across the whole garden of dreams. Of course, it is greeted with the usual amount of debate, profound disagreements about its truth, insightful deliberations about its lies.

There is even one school of thought that claims it could come true, if you believed.

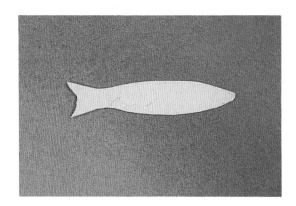

Groundwood Books/Douglas & McIntyre Ltd.
585 Bloor Street West
Toronto, Ontario M6G 1K5

The publisher gratefully acknowledges the assis-
tance of the Canada Council, the Ontario Arts
Council and the Ontario Ministry of Culture,
Tourism and Recreation.

Canadian Cataloguing in Publication Data

Yerxa, Leo, 1947-
A fish tale, or, The little one that got away

ISBN 0-88899-247-5

I. Title. II. Title: The little one that got away.

PS8597.E77F5 1995   jC813'.54   C95-931522-5
PZ7.Y47Fi 1995

The illustrations are done in watercolors and
stenciled pastels
Design by Michael Solomon
Printed and bound in Hong Kong by
Everbest Printing Co. Ltd.